THE SEASIDE STORYBOOK IS DEDICATED TO THE READERS

"ENJOY YOUR CHILDHOOD WHILE YOU CAN."
CASH WATSON

"From pirates to sprites to kittens in the night, The Seaside Storybook offers creative gems from the insightful teen authors of Carlsbad Seaside Academy."
Kiesa Kay, class encourager

Thank you, Hannah Carroll, Emma Stokes, Marelyn Catano, Maddie Wernig, Aaron Love, and Eilish Friestman. Your phenomenal editing, illustration, and formatting made The Seaside Storybook more than just a classroom dream. Your talent, creativity, and diligence carried our children's book to the finish line of publication. I see epic success in your lives and look forward to cheering you along the way. I also can't forget my principal, Mr. Espinoza, coworker, Shannon Schmitt, and CSA Staff, for assisting students in writing and publishing The Seaside Storybook.

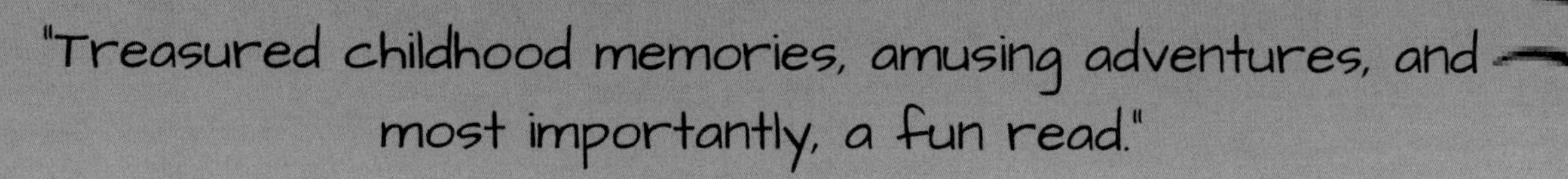

"Treasured childhood memories, amusing adventures, and most importantly, a fun read."

FELIX BUENO

"Reflective, comedic, mournful, joyous-a compilation of what teenagers wish to impart to the next generation."

MAIZIE ZARLING

"Students put much thought and effort into each story to create a storybook they would have wanted to read when they were younger."

CHARLOTTE CLIFF

The Seaside Storybook
By Carlsbad Seaside Academy Students
Published by Warrior Publishing
Print ISBN:: 979-8-9881366-3-7

Cover Design by Hannah Carroll
Available in print format

Contact the author via email at savingsummersuzyryan@gmail.com.

Printed in the United States of America

Seventh and Eighth Grade

A Sweet Dream

WRITTEN AND ILLUSTRATED BY AARON LOVE

Throughout the landscape, an array of sugary delights could be found
From a candy cane woodland boasting hues of ruby and white,
To rocky road mountains, cascading their velvety chocolate toward the ground,
Over the rolling hills of frosted cake that glistened in rainbow light.

Between the valleys of layered fudge where fresh milk was streaming
Past fields of vibrant, chewy jelly sweets and gummies.
In the center stood a young boy, his face gleaming.
For many minutes, the child ventured, empowered by his tummy.

After almost satisfying his cravings, he felt a tug as if on a string.
To the west, the invisible line pulled him closer with each footprint
Through the meadows of lollipops and saltwater taffy radiating like flowers
In the spring around the marshland of swaying marshmallows
With their golden s'more tint.

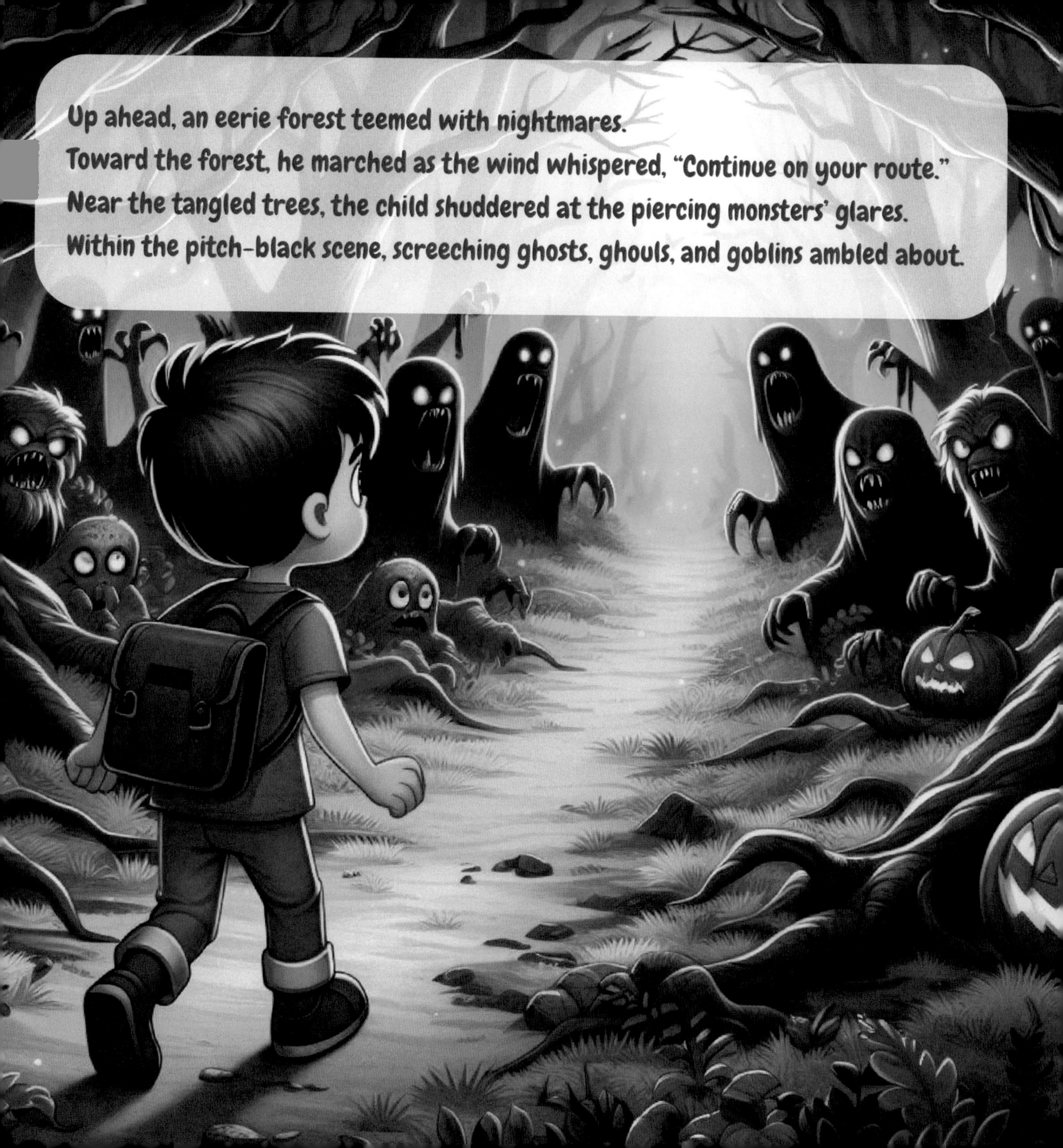
Up ahead, an eerie forest teemed with nightmares.
Toward the forest, he marched as the wind whispered, "Continue on your route."
Near the tangled trees, the child shuddered at the piercing monsters' glares.
Within the pitch-black scene, screeching ghosts, ghouls, and goblins ambled about.

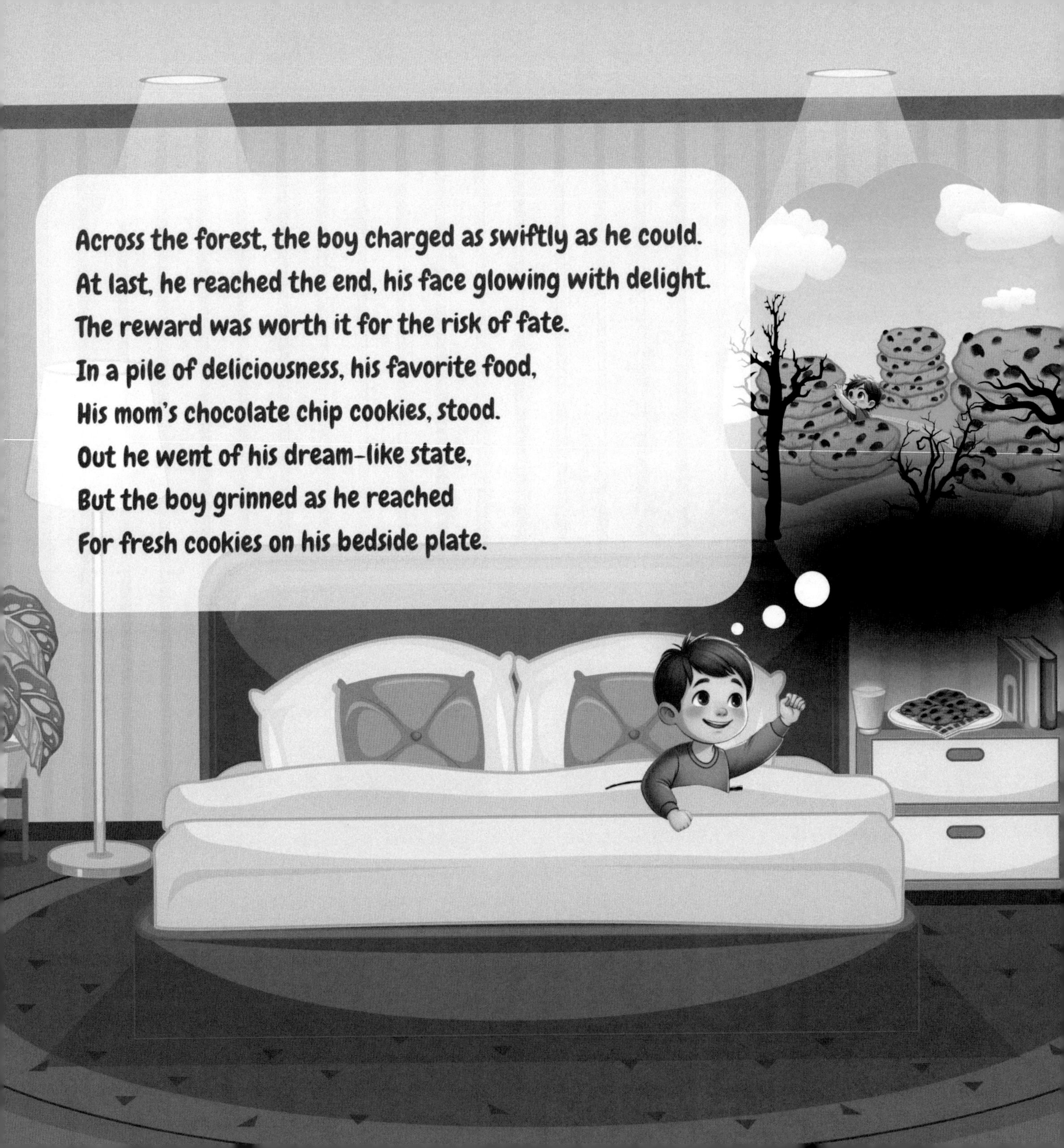

Across the forest, the boy charged as swiftly as he could.
At last, he reached the end, his face glowing with delight.
The reward was worth it for the risk of fate.
In a pile of deliciousness, his favorite food,
His mom's chocolate chip cookies, stood.
Out he went of his dream-like state,
But the boy grinned as he reached
For fresh cookies on his bedside plate.

Stage Fright

WRITTEN BY KEIRA SEGAL AND
ILLUSTRATED BY GWEN DAYNES

As she twirls with her leg up high
So beautiful to the judge's eye
She leaps and bounds with such grace
She is sure to take first place

But unfortunately, she isn't me
As I watch backstage nervously
Next, it will be my turn
I pace around as my stomach churns

The sound of clapping fills the air
My heart stops, time to prepare
I walk on stage to face my fear
My friends and family start to cheer

As I do the most exquisite dance
I feel that I'm in a trance
My body suddenly feels at home
The stage feels like my safe zone

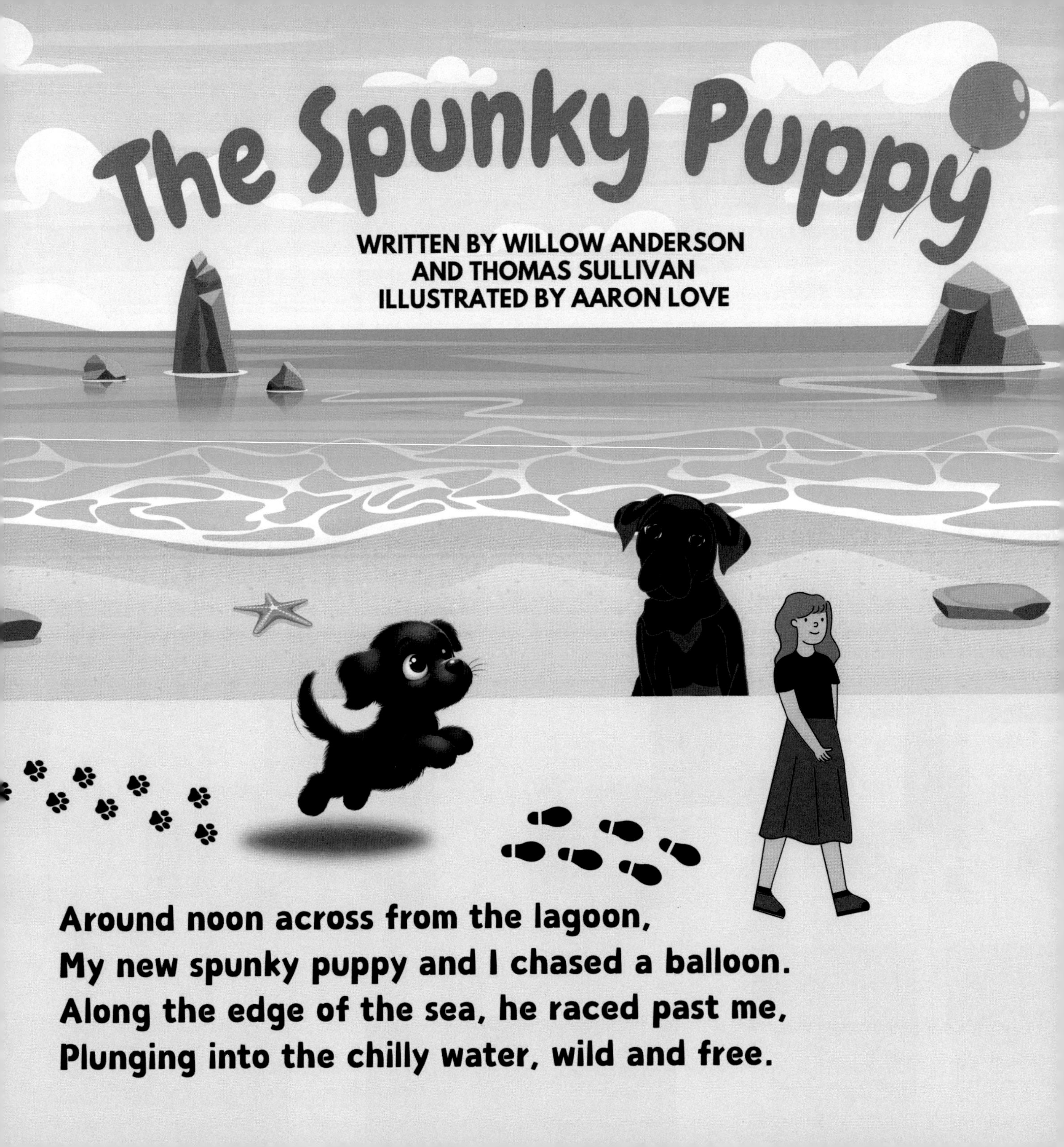

The Spunky Puppy

WRITTEN BY WILLOW ANDERSON
AND THOMAS SULLIVAN
ILLUSTRATED BY AARON LOVE

**Around noon across from the lagoon,
My new spunky puppy and I chased a balloon.
Along the edge of the sea, he raced past me,
Plunging into the chilly water, wild and free.**

At once, we formed an
Unbreakable bond,
And of him, I grew
Extremely fond.

Because this little
Puppy and I, you see,
Were forever and
Always, meant to be.

Now, I'm plenty lucky
To call my newfound
Buddy, my beloved
Spunky Puppy.

Little World of Fall

WRITTEN AND ILLUSTRATED BY
CARTER JUDE DAU AND JACK HOULIHAN

When the sky was gloomy, but all was still aglow
Hundreds of trees sat surrounded by patches of snow
This world of pine stood still and quiet
As all you could hear
Was the sound of time
Time, that ticks on
Moving forward and
Hopping along
But when wind whistles
Through, we start to hear
Things that we undervalue

The slight squeaks of a squirrel hiding in fear
From an owl that watches near
Perching upon a tree wide-eyed and filled with glee
A deer casually prances by
Walking carefully through the fields of orange and white
His mind is set on a valley that lays close and in sight
This sacred place of vibrant colors and misty mountains
Is just around the corner although
Nobody seems to look
This little world unseen by all
Just happens to be the
Most beautiful in the fall

The Hullabaloo At the Zoo

WRITTEN BY BENJAMIN HANSINK
AND PAIGE MCCONNELL
ILLUSTRATED BY AARON LOVE

IN THE HEART OF SAN DIEGO, THERE LIVED FOUR FRIENDS—LANCE THE LION, GERRY THE GIRAFFE, ZIPPY THE ZEBRA, AND PETER THE PANDA—WHO ALL MISSED THEIR PARENTS BACK HOME ON THE VERANDA.

ONE DAY AS IT HAPPENED, AFTER A DAPENED DOWNPOUR IN THE PANDA DEN, PETER STASHED BAMBOO SHOOTS, DASHED FOR THE FENCE, AND SAID.

"I'VE JUST GOT TO SEE MY MOM AN DAD AGAIN."

PERCEPTIVE PAIGE, WHO WORKED AT THE ZOO, PROMPTLY FOLLOWED THE HOMESICK PANDA AS HE CHEWED ON BAMBOO.

WITH A MAGNIFYING GLASS IN HAND, PAIGE ENCOURAGED PETER TO BE GLAD. "TOMORROW, YOUR MOM AND DAD ARE SURPRISE GUESTS FROM A FAR-AWAY LAND,

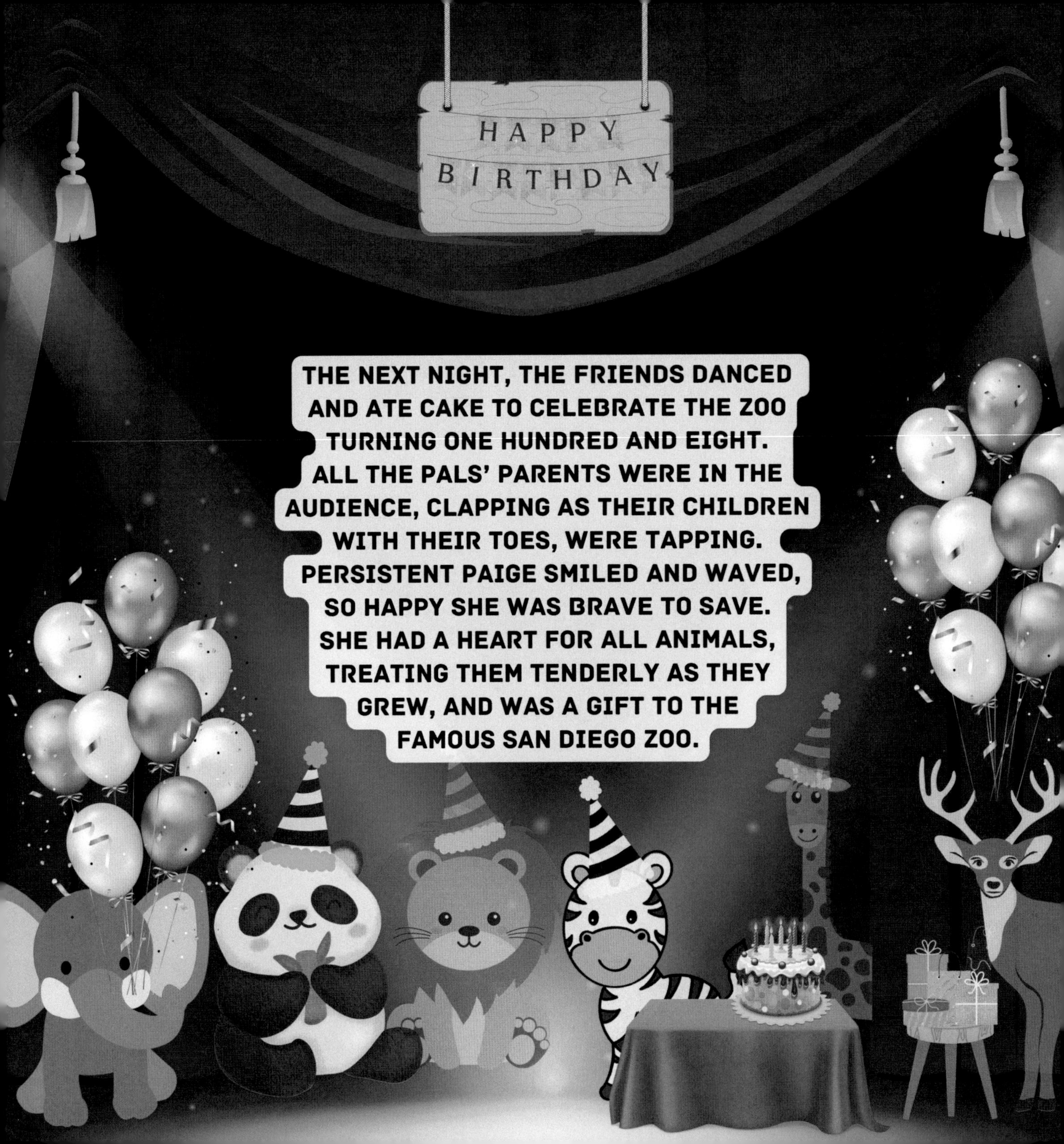

THE NEXT NIGHT, THE FRIENDS DANCED AND ATE CAKE TO CELEBRATE THE ZOO TURNING ONE HUNDRED AND EIGHT. ALL THE PALS' PARENTS WERE IN THE AUDIENCE, CLAPPING AS THEIR CHILDREN WITH THEIR TOES, WERE TAPPING. PERSISTENT PAIGE SMILED AND WAVED, SO HAPPY SHE WAS BRAVE TO SAVE. SHE HAD A HEART FOR ALL ANIMALS, TREATING THEM TENDERLY AS THEY GREW, AND WAS A GIFT TO THE FAMOUS SAN DIEGO ZOO.

Fear is a Fibber

WRITTEN BY MRS. RYAN
ILLUSTRATED BY HANNAH CARROLL

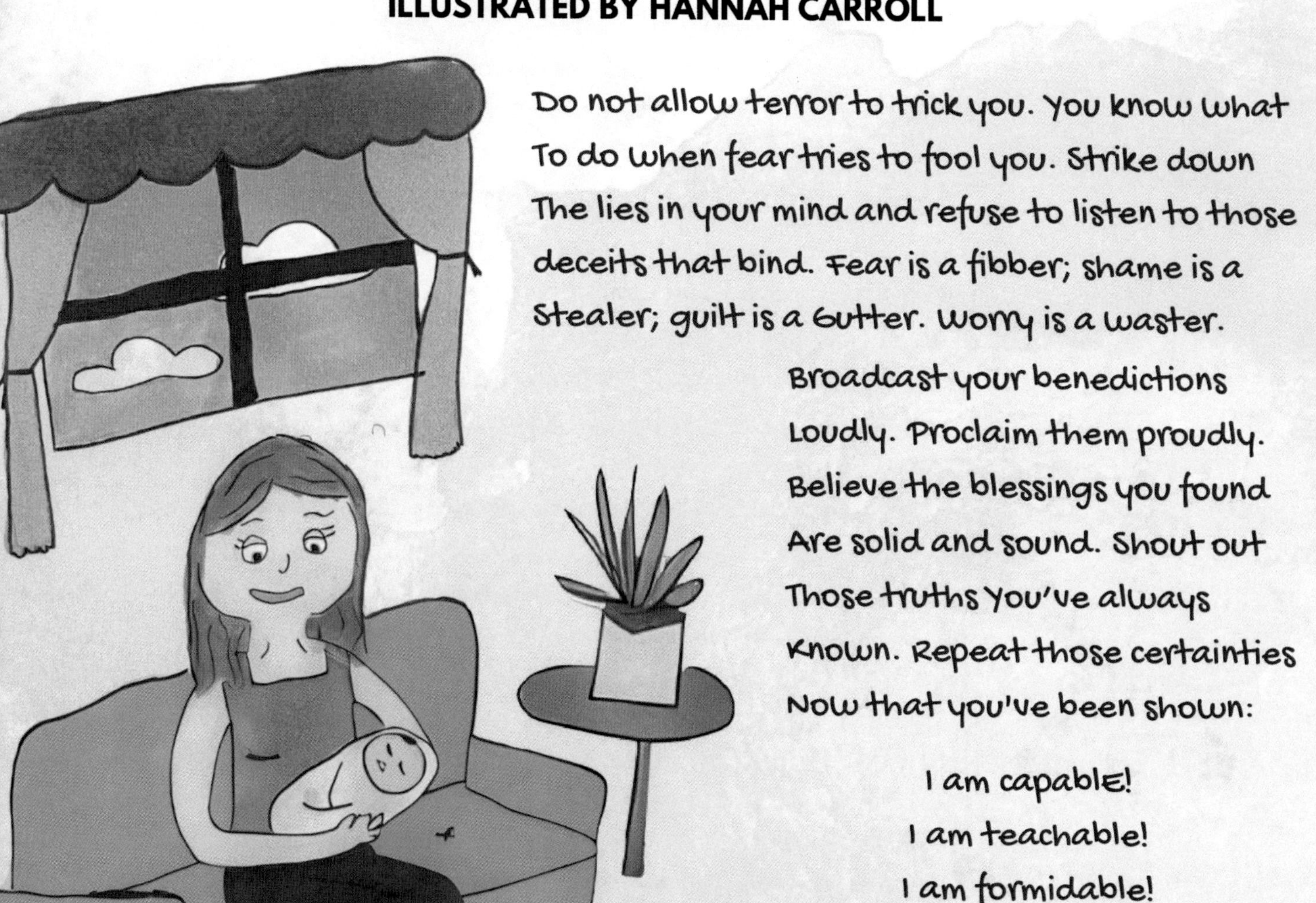

Do not allow terror to trick you. You know what
To do when fear tries to fool you. Strike down
The lies in your mind and refuse to listen to those
deceits that bind. Fear is a fibber; shame is a
Stealer; guilt is a Gutter. Worry is a waster.

Broadcast your benedictions
Loudly. Proclaim them proudly.
Believe the blessings you found
Are solid and sound. Shout out
Those truths You've always
Known. Repeat those certainties
Now that you've been shown:

I am capable!
I am teachable!
I am formidable!
I am valuable!

I am more than able to stare fear in the face and say,
"Now it is time for you, Fear, to get off my case."

Take His Hand

WRITTEN AND ILLUSTRATED BY BROOKLYN PAYNE

As people live their lives, I watch from above.
Reaching out My hand to help them walk on water.
"Why are You helping? You know I've sinned countless times."
"I am forgiving," God said to my heart.
"Now, give me your hands. I will guide you through your plans."

God does not judge, despite your acts;
He simply leans down and tells you to relax.

For He will take problems away,
So you can digest the day and hit the hay.

Take His hand and let Him guide you.
He knows you inside and out. Don't push Him away.

Let Him show you the light He can make.
Breathe. Take His hand and be relieved.

With your hand in HIs, you can reach beyond.
He is crazy fond of you, only desiring a bond.

You Are Smart

WRITTEN AND ILLUSTRATED BY EMMA STOKES

Am I smart?
What does it mean
to be smart?
Does smart mean building
a house?
Does it mean sewing
a blouse?
Does it mean solving
tough math?
Does it mean hitting
a ball with a bat?

Writing a story, maybe?
Or taking care of a baby?
Is it getting a car to start?
Or warming someone's heart?
Could it be healing
Someone who's ill?
Or cooking yummy
Food on a grill?
Maybe baking a
delicious cake?
Or learning from your
mistakes?

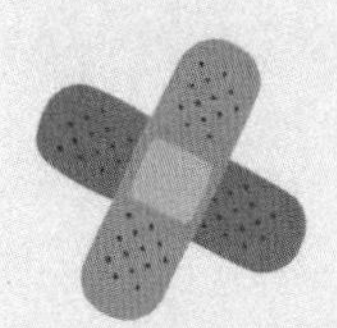

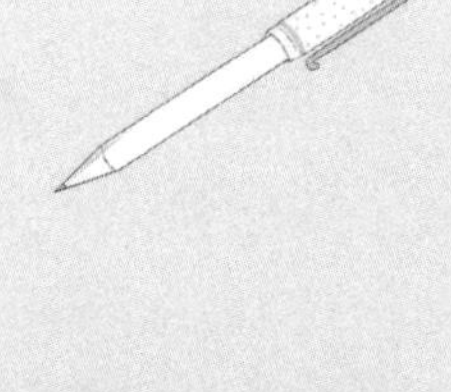

You Are Smart

Never be afraid to
be curious,
That's how you're truly
victorious!
It can sometimes feel
scary and tough,
But give it your all!
That's smart enough.

TWILIGHT AT THE PIER

WRITTEN AND ILLUSTRATED BY
MAX OLSCHEWSKI AND JORDY NOVELL

As the sun dips low, the sky painted gold,
A seaside pier tale, forever to be told.
Whispers of waves, a lullaby so sweet,
As the day and the horizon finally meet.
Seagulls in silhouette, dance in the light,
Their wings carry stories, taking flight.
Colors blend in a colorful pallet,
An ocean symphony at the closing of day.
Boardwalk echoes with footsteps light,
A serene hush settles, a calmly lit night.
Sunset hues linger, a warm embrace,
Nature's masterpiece, a tranquil grace.
On the seaside pier, where time stands still,
A sunset serenade, a moment to fulfill.
The horizon's glow, a celestial fire,
In the twilight's calm, dreams do aspire.

Alone Together

WRITTEN AND ILLUSTRATED BY REBEKAH SARRIS

Beneath the sorrow
Beautiful as a shimmering jewel
furled in the tapestry of existence

Warrior with a zealous heart
Hair with waves of pure earth
Softly reflecting the light of the sun
The start of a new chapter

If you hear bells ringing
You will see yourself crying
Beautiful eyes with the shine of
Emeralds stinging you take the pain of others
And then carry it inside you

But you know the truth
Moving forward isn't for everyone
The only way is through
You can't even get out of a wretched door
But one day, one time, you will succeed
You can grow, take your things, and leave
But you feel like a monster throwing yourself
In a cage that covers the road with snow
You can grow

I will be the fire and the cold winter shelter
I will not have to be told
I will be the light you searched for
I will be what you breathe
I will understand what you have inside
I will be the drinking water

I will be beside you, the meaning of good
I will be laughter or the light in the evening
I will run a mile in your shoes
And in return, I ask for nothing

Just a smile
Beautiful as the sun
You lost the fruit of your womb
You have not found the one
They told you there
Is a castle in the city
With such powerful walls
That if you go live inside
Nothing can batter
You anymore

Dream, Kid! Dream!

WRITTEN BY NOAH MENDLES ELLIOTT
ILLUSTRATED BY EMMA STOKES

I once was scared to dream, the ominous
Monsters I imagined made me scream!

Like some ghosts with their spooky shapes,
They would scratch and scrape.

Some would have a lime-green hue
And that scared me, too.

But now I am no longer afraid
Because I realize life is a parade.

You can either be
Scared since you were born
Or enjoy life and eat popcorn.

As a wise person once told me
When I blew off steam,
Dream, Kid! Dream!

Tom and Jerry's Adventure

WRITTEN BY SAMMY YOSUFI

ILLUSTRATED BY EMMA BOLL AND MARELYN CATANO

"JERRY, CAN YOU BELIEVE MY GIRL KEEPS TRYING TO PICK ME UP?" TOM, THE GREY, FAT CAT SAID. "YOU'D THINK BY MY CONSTANT MEOWING, MY OWNER WOULD KNOW I'VE GOT OTHER THINGS TO DO. AT LEAST YOUR GIRL LEAVES YOU ALONE."

"NOT WHEN MY GIRL AND I NAP," JERRY,
THE BROWN-STRIPED, FLABBY, TABBY CAT ANSWERED.
"I LOVE IT WHEN SHE PUTS ME ON HER LAP."
"IF SHE CAN EVEN LIFT YOU," TOM HISSED.
"LAY OFF THE TREATS, WILL YOU, BROTHER?
YOU'RE GETTING A LITTLE CHUNKY."
"HAVE YOU LOOKED IN THE MIRROR?" JERRY MEOWED,
HIS HAZEL EYES SQUINTING.
"BOTH OUR TUMMIES MIGHT EXPLODE. BUT HEY, AT LEAST
OUR BIG BELLIES ARE HIDDEN WITH FUR—UNLESS OUR
GIRLS TRY TO SHAVE US."

"I DOUBT THAT WOULD HAPPEN, THEY LOVE OUR FUZZY FUR," TOM SAID, SCRATCHING HIS ENORMOUS WHITE TUMMY, "EVEN IF THEY DID SHAVE US, WHO CARES? AS LONG AS THEY FEED US. FOOD IS MY LIFE!"

"ARE YOU KIDDING? FOOD ISN'T EVERYTHING—MY FANTASTIC FUR IS!" JERRY ARCHED HIS BACK. IF I EVEN SEE MY GIRL TOUCH THE CLIPPERS, I'M JUMPING OFF OF THE BALCONY. BUT IT'S OKAY. I HAVE NINE LIVES."

"ARE YOU DREAMING, LITTLE BROTHER?" TOM BIT JERRY ON THE BUTT. "THAT NINE LIVES BUSINESS IS A HOAX. YOU ONLY HAVE ONE."

JERRY CHASED TOM TO THE BALCONY, HIS BROWNISH-GREEN EYES AGLOW. "LOOK OUT!" JERRY SAID AS TOM VAULTED OVER HIS BROTHER, LANDING ON THE BRONZE RAILING. TOM PRANCED HIS WHITE PAWS ACROSS THE EDGE AND LOOKED OVER HIS SHOULDER. JERRY'S GIRL RACED TOWARD HER CAT WITH THE CLIPPERS.

"JERRY! WATCH OUT!" TOM YELLED TO HIS BROTHER, HIS TAIL PUFFING UP—HIS PUPILS WIDENING.

"HURRY, JERRY! JUUUUMP! I'LL JUMP WITH YOUUUUUU!"

Ninth and Tenth Grade

Natural Natur
Marathon
WRITTEN AND ILLUSTRATED BY AUTUMN NORRINGTON
40
25
10
GO
RUNNERS!
My sister, dad, and I
Tramped through the trails.
Along came the rugged
Runners, we were right on
Their tails!
Intense music ran in our
Ears, filling us with all the
People's cheers.
I didn't know about this
Event, though. I've been
Livin' here for years!

The air smelled of fresh pine trees, flowing through the breeze. This walk made me feel pleased.
We also brought along our dog.
Gosh, good thing the weather didn't have fog!

The Broken Board

WRITTEN AND ILLUSTRATED BY NATE WEITZ AND FELIX BUENO

On the train that takes us far, we pass
The highway full of cars to downtown
Where the buildings are tall and where
People there feel small

When we hop off, we see the lights of the
Beautiful city of San Diego at night, and
On this night, we're about to have an
Epic fright

We skated around Old Town until the
Incident went down, flying high, wind
Flowing through my hair, I hit a kickflip
A trick so fair

After landing from the air, I looked
Down at my board in despair, It lay
Snapped on the ground, my face
Formed into a frown

My perfect deck was gone in a flash
The only action I could take was to
Throw it in the trash

On the train home, in the pitch black
I decided to give myself some slack
Because good tends to come after bad
And it is never worth being sad

Enjoy Your Childhood

WRITTEN AND ILLUSTRATED BY CASH WATSON

In his happy place, a home filled with glee
Lived a surfer kid, blissful as could be

Awakened, ready for a day so cool
Excited to start, no need for school

Downstairs, his parents beamed with delight
Kid was jolly, sipping a sprite

He packed the car and
Grabbed his key

He was on the road
Wild and free

Windows down, music
Loud, what a trip

Drove to the beach
Ready to rip

Waves breaking at
Perfect height

Ready for a surf
Feeling just right

Watching the waves
Gearing up to go

Paddling out
Oh, the ocean's sweet flow

Duck diving a wave
Feeling the wave's power

Sitting on my board
Ready to paddle

As waves rise and fall with a
Smooth sway

I wait with anticipation
Eager to play

With a surge of adrenaline
I paddle and crave

A moment of bliss as I catch
The next wave

Above the water
Nearly touching the sky

Riding the crest
Feeling free to fly

Completing the wave
Ready for another ride

I embrace the sea
I'll always comply

Friends on the beach
Laughter in the sand

A day in the life
With memories so grand

Tuxy, King of the Cats

WRITTEN AND ILLUSTRATED BY CRUZ DOUGLASS

THE MORNING SUN ROSE, AND DOWN WENT THE MOON,
THE LIGHTHOUSE AND BOAT DOCK WOULD OPEN UP SOON.
WITH A STRETCH AND A PURR, A BLACK MOUND WOULD RISE,
WHO HAD GAZED MANY STARS, AND SEEN MANY SKIES.

TUXY KEPT THE LIGHTHOUSE AND GREETED THE SHORE.
A WHITE AND GREY CAT SAILED THE BOAT "EVERMORE"
WITH BEAUTIFUL COLORS, APPLEJACK WAS HIS NAME,
A GENTLE GIANT SO SHY, BUT WHO LIKED TO PLAY GAMES.
TUXY SHOWED HIM A COMPASS AND THE CAT VENTURED OFF,
APPLEJACK LEFT TUXY ALONE AT THE DOCK.

IT WASNT LONG BEFORE A CAT
WASHED ASHORE JUST THE SAME,
A SMALL MAMMA MIA, A VERY SWEET DAME.
SHE HUNTED THE RATS AND JUMPED IN THE HAY,
BUT SOON SHE WOULD RIDE OFF TOWARD LOVELY BAY.

SOON A STORM ROSE AND WASHED UP ASHORE,
A SCAREDY CAT THUMPER HID UNDER THE FLOOR.
THE LIGHTHOUSE HAD FALLEN, A HURRICANE NEAR,
THUNDER SCARED TUXY AND HE RAN IN FEAR.

AS THE SUN STARTED TO SET, ANOTHER CAT ARRIVED,
A CAT DARK AS NIGHT BOUNDED THROUGH THE SEA TIDE.
BUZZ WAS A GIANT, JUST LIKE APPLEJACK,
HE PLAYED WITH TUXY RUNNING DOWN AND BACK.
WHEN HE WAS LEAVING, HE LET TUXY ON HIS BOAT,
HE PACKED UP HIS THINGS AND WAS READY TO GO.

THEY WENT PAST AN ISLAND COVERED IN THE SNOW,
WITH A FURBALL MISS MOONIE SNUGGLED BELOW.

SOON THUNDER ROLLED IN, WITH A FLASH OF LIGHT,
BUT A FLASH OF ORANGE KITTEN ZOOMED INTO SIGHT.
THE FOURTH ON THE BOAT, A SMALL ONE AT THAT,
THE SPEEDY PUFF DADDY WAS A PLAYFUL CAT.

SOON THE BOAT ARRIVED AT A BEACH.
BIRDS FLEW IN CIRCLES HOLDING SHELLS IN THEIR BEAKS.

A CASTLE WAS GREY AND PEARLY WHITE.
AN ABANDONED KINGDOM WITH NO KING IN SIGHT.

SO AS LONG AS THE CASTLE HAD ONE OR TWO RATS,
TUXY WOULD STILL BE KING OF THE CATS.

TOKYO TALES

WRITTEN AND ILLUSTRATED BY CHANNAH BURGOYNE

In Tokyo town, where lights gleam bright,
A city of wonders, both day and night.
Skyscrapers soar, reaching the sky,
Amidst the bustle, where dreams can fly.

Trains trundle through
The town,
Tokyo Tower,
Wearing its crown.
Towering trees
In tranquil parks,
Tales of serenity,
Where light sparks.

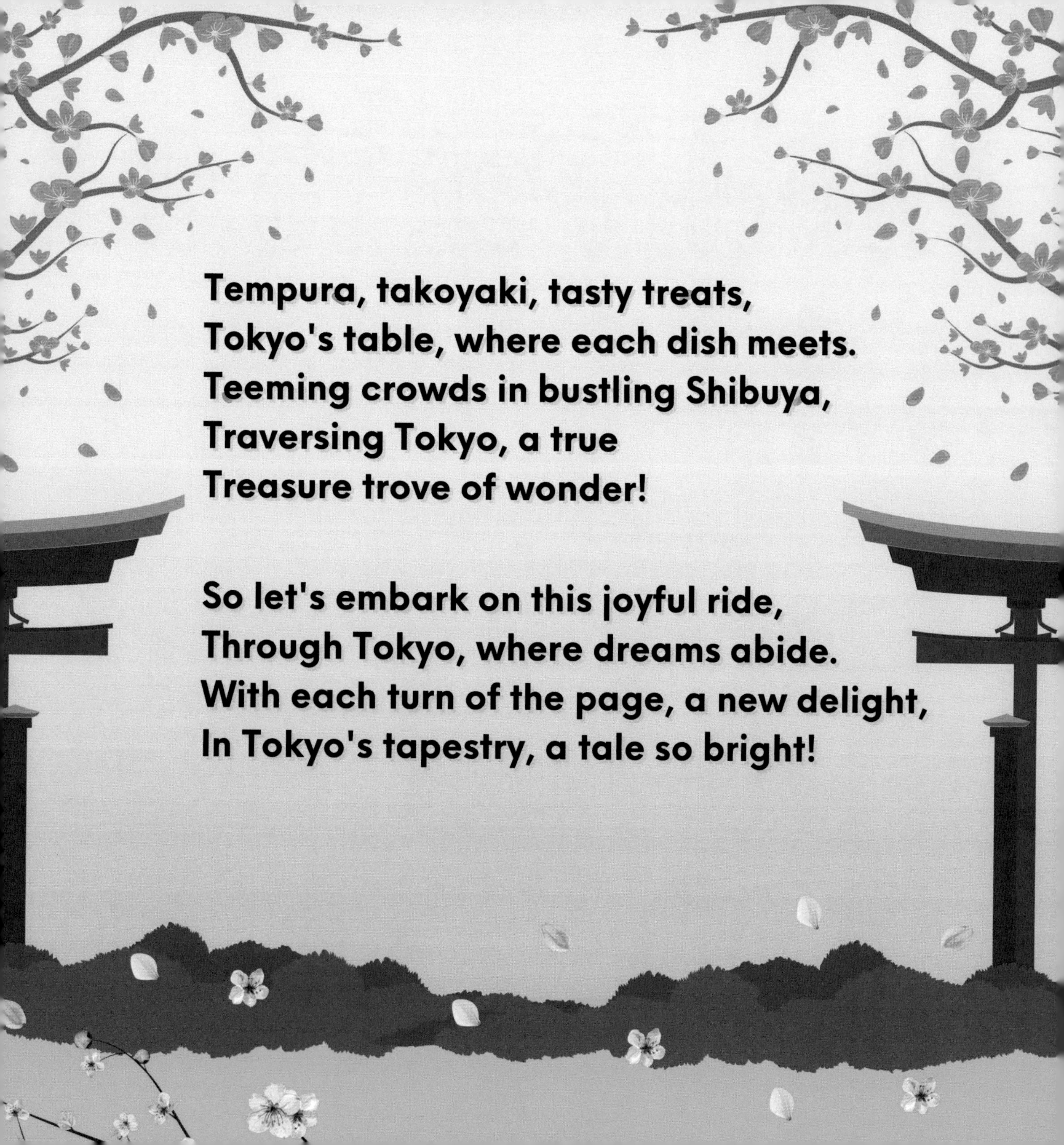

Tempura, takoyaki, tasty treats,
Tokyo's table, where each dish meets.
Teeming crowds in bustling Shibuya,
Traversing Tokyo, a true
Treasure trove of wonder!

So let's embark on this joyful ride,
Through Tokyo, where dreams abide.
With each turn of the page, a new delight,
In Tokyo's tapestry, a tale so bright!

Which Pet To Get

WRITTEN AND ILLUSTRATED BY
EVERETT CASTANEDA
AND LUKE MACBETH

MATEO WAS SURE THAT HE WANTED A PET.
HE TALKED TO HIS DAD ABOUT WHICH PET TO GET.

HE SAID, "I WANT A MONKEY WHO SCRATCHES HIS HEAD.
WHO WILL SWING OFF THE HOUSE AND JUMP ONTO THE BED."

"WELL," SAID HIS DAD IN A KIND SORT OF WAY.
"DID YOU KNOW THAT MONKEYS EAT BUGS EVERY SINGLE DAY?"

"OH!" MATEO SAID, "HE WILL HAVE NOTHING TO EAT.
BECAUSE MOM LIKES TO SQUASH ALL THE BUGS UNDER HER FEET."

"THEN I WANT A HIPPO!" MATEO SCREAMED TO HIS DAD.
"HE'D EAT ALL OF OUR TRASH, AND MOM WOULD BE GLAD!"

"HIPPOS NEED WATER, SON. IT HELPS THEM TO STAY COOL.
WE CAN BUILD HIM A GIANT-SIZED, UNDERGROUND POOL."

"NO!" MATEO SAID, "HE'D BE TOO BIG TO DRY.
WE'D NEED A HUGE MOUNTAIN OF TOWELS TO EVEN TRY."

"THEN I WANT AN OTTER," MATEO SCREECHED TO HIS DAD,
"I BET HIS TRIPLE BACKFLIPS WILL BE INCREDIBLY RAD."

"DID YOU KNOW," DAD SAID. "MOST OTTERS CAN WHISTLE AND CHIRP?
THEY GROWL AND SNORT, AND PERHAPS EVEN BURP."

"OH," MATEO SAID WITH A SAD-FACED FROWN,
"WE'D HAVE TO TELL HIM TO KEEP THE NOISE DOWN."

AT THE NEWS, MATEO HUNG HIS HEAD LOW.
THEN WITH A HOPEFUL SMILE, HE SAID, "NOW THAT I KNOW,

PLEASE ANSWER ONLY ONE QUESTION, THEN I'LL HAVE NO REGRETS.
HOW ARE LITTLE BROTHERS FOR EVERYDAY PETS?"

The Best Day Ever

WRITTEN AND ILLUSTRATED
BY HANNAH CARROLL

At the top of the mountain,
Through the snowy slopes,
Across the deep powder,
I dragged my sled by the ropes.
Before the run, shivering with
Anticipation and hope,
My cousins and I gazed down
At what we wanted most.

Bundled up in our warmest clothes,
We tumbled into the toboggan
And got ready to go.

After a push, the sled slid slowly
Across the snow, and just like that,
We could see more of what was below.
Faster and faster, we held onto the
Edge of the sled,
Snow was flying
Everywhere, in my
Face, and all over my
Head. Like no other,
Our speed careened
Out of control,
Until we toppled off, landing
In a wacky pose after a roll.
Heading back into the cabin
To watch Christmas shows,
We all agreed, it was the
Best day ever in the snow.

The Seal Scare

WRITTEN AND ILLUSTRATED BY
HOLLAND FULLER AND TY SHAVER

GOING DOWN TO THE BEACH, MY FRIENDS BY MY SIDE.
WE RACE TO THE WATER AND PADDLE OUTSIDE.

FAR OUT PAST THE BREAK, WE SIT AND WAIT
FOR THE PERFECT WAVE, WE WANT TO TAKE.

THEN SOMEWHERE FROM THE OCEAN DEEP,
UP TO THE SURFACE, WITH BIG, SHINING TEETH

A SEAL BREAKS FREE,
LEAPING TOWARD ME.

OVER 200 POUNDS COMES DOWN FROM THE SKY.
WITH HIS SMALL HEAD AND LARGE EYES,
I WANTED TO CRY.

AS THE SEAL KISSES MY HEAD.
I DON'T FEEL ANY DREAD.

BACK ON THE BEACH, PONDERING THE PAST.
SCARY AS IT WAS, THE FEAR DID NOT LAST.

YOU MAY DOUBT MY STORY.
THIS SEAL DISPLAYED SUCH GLORY.

NEXT TIME YOU RIDE A WAVE,
MAKE SURE YOU ARE BRAVE.

THEN A LEOPARD-SPOTTED MARINE MAMMAL
YOU JUST MAY SEE,
AND HAVE THE SAME PHENOMENAL FATE AS ME!

Whispers of the Soul

WRITTEN AND ILLUSTRATED BY
JOSHUA SHERMAN

In the shadows of the mind, where our thoughts
Reside within our hearts, behind a mask we hide.
Beneath the surface, our feelings start to sway.
Among all the whispers, darkness holds us captive.
Through the hallways of confusion, feeling lost we
Roam amidst our struggles, longing for a way
Back home. Behind the laughter, our silence cries.
Above the chaos, with heavy sighs.

Under the weight of expectations,
We bear the pain. Amidst the storm, we long for
Love to remain. Across the pages of our thoughts,
Our tales unfold.

Against the current, our resilience molds. Upon
The journey, we'll persevere. With every step, we
Conquer our fear. Within our hearts, a flame
Ignites beneath the stars, where hope alights.

A Pirate's Worst Nightmare

WRITTEN AND ILLUSTRATED BY JACOB KAHANE

Beneath the waves, the treasure was found.
The hidden gem lay safe and sound.

At the heart of Carlsbad, right by the sea,
A pirate ship was spotted for all to see.
The village quickly rushed to take a look,
To see the pirate's arm with only a hook.

Hundreds of pirates came
Out of the bay, swinging
Their swords, to slay their prey.

Yet mighty Max, with the gem in hand,
Stepped forward, to take a bold stand.
He had the ocean's gift, so brave and rare.
Everyone could only stop and stare.

The pirates listened,
Backing off to the gentle waves.
That day no one was imprisoned.
The town cheered and gave Max praise.

Thirst

WRITTEN AND ILLUSTRATED
BY KALEB MILLER

In the middle of the desert,
While feeling like nothing could be hotter,

I trudged my way through the dunes,
In the search of any water.

At last, after what had seemed like hours,
I noticed an oasis rich in flowers.

I ran through the sand, wanting to
Quench my thirst, while hoping no
One had gotten there first.

After drinking the stagnant water,
My stomach started to rumble.

I threw up everywhere; my insides
Cramped, making me crumble.

When I returned to my hideout
On the hill, I knew to never again
Drink water that had been sitting still.

From Me to You

WRITTEN BY BROOKLYN DILLON
ILLUSTRATED BY EILISH FRIESTMAN

Change is the only constant in life
You might as well learn to adapt
No matter how much you love
Something, it will change
The past may seem so much "better"
The future may look intimidating
The present may not be "good enough"
Change is losing someone
The distance grows uncomfortable
You can no longer talk to them with ease
You dread interactions
As time moves forward
Guilt and regret abound

Change may feel scary
You may have questions
You may ponder what
Tomorrow will bring

Still, many changes
occur for the better
They can lead to the greatest good
Resilience and strength emerge
Change is the only constant
We might as well learn to adapt

Out The Window, My Cat Flew
WRITTEN AND ILLUSTRATED
BY KEIRA SWEENEY

Inside by the window, perched on a stand,
Out flew my cat, on her feet, I hoped she'd land.
At first, my family did surmise,
Through the open screen, she fell to her demise.

When sunrise came, I decided to search,
And I posted some flyers at a nearby church.
I searched high and low and everywhere she could be,
Riveted on bringing her back home to me.

I questioned the locals if Riley had been seen,
My missed fluffy ball of fur that had gone unseen.
About two weeks later, we thought all was lost,
We wanted Riley home at any cost.

Then a miracle happened by our mailbox that night,
There stood a lady with a wondrous sight.
In her arms, she held our precious Miss Riley,
Instantly, my mom and I were now all smiley.

Our cat was finally brought back home,
We will keep her inside, so she shall never again roam.

Keira

Little Critter

WRITTEN BY
KATY MEDWAY
ILLUSTRATED BY
JULIETA PAREJA
AND LILY IRVINE

Over mountains
Under trees
Rests a little critter hard to see.

He has wings, scales
horns, and tails!

Little critter jumps, swings and flies
Over mountains
Under trees
Through skies.

"Stop!" say the giants in the clouds.
"Stop!" say the elves in the forest.

"Little critter! You're flying too high!
Come down to the seashore, so you don't die."

"I have wings, scales
horns and tails!
Yet I come down to the seashore
From over mountains
Under trees
I descend."

"Psst!! Come here, my friend!"
"Who are you?"

"You will see
Once you walk closer to me!"

Little Critter jumps,
Swings and flies
Closer to the voice
Where a little girl cries.

"My toy!
It flew away in the breeze!
It's at the peak of Mt. Grashesbit
Where it awaits before something
Smashes it!"

Little Critter jumps,
Swings and flies
Over mountains
Under trees
Through skies.

"Stop!" say the giants in the clouds.
"Stop!" say the elves in the forest.

"Little Critter!
You're flying too high!
Come down to the seashore!
Don't even try!"

But Little Critter keeps going.
He doesn't blink an eye.
Little Critter flies to the peak of
Mt. Grashesbit.

A toy sparkles, shimmers and
Shines, so Little Critter swoops
Down before something smashes it.

Little Critter jumps,
Swings and flies
Above the seashore.
He spots the little girl.

Little Critter gives the little girl her
Toy, her face glows with joy.

Little Critter takes flight
Over mountains
Under trees
Into the night.

THE TRUTH ABOUT TIME

WRITTEN AND ILLUSTRATED BY
MADELINE WERNIG

Time doesn't speed up or slow down for those
With wealth, knowledge, or power.
Time is uncontrollable. It can't be altered
By a second, a minute, or even an hour.

The truth about time is that it governs our
Lives. But time reminds you, "The ultimate
Winner is the one who continually strives."

Time's tempo is fast and then slow.
Just take it one day at a time and go with
The flow. Sometimes, you may worry the
Clock is ticking, but remember, time isn't
What you're seeking.

The truth about time is that to win the race,
You have to take a deep breath and slow
Down your pace.

Time may try to trick you, making you think
You're too slow, but if you keep a cool head,
You'll be sure to be in the know.
To win against time, you must be present in
The moment. And remember, wasting time is
The real opponent.

Time is a gift, precious and dear, a passage to
Cherish, year after year, time helps you find
What you are seeking, making you grow,
Guiding you through life's highest highs and
Lowest lows.

The truth about time is that it's worth more
Than gold. So value your time, and remember
What you've been told. Time is a tremendous
Tool you can use, something unique,
Something you don't want to lose.

Invisible Thief

WRITTEN AND ILLUSTRATED
BY MAIZIE ZARLING

To live is to be stolen from
By the invisible thief
Not malicious nor greedy
Yet leaves you empty inside
Filled with grief

For a moment, you will find
The belief you can run away
From her. Still lies buried deep
Inside. In your room, dollhouse
On display, Pots and pans,
The ultimate object of play

Into your mind, she goes
Taking what you call home
Through the windows of time
She travels, altering all that is known

Beneath the veil of her false name
As much as she steals, she returns
"Thief" no longer sounds quite the
Same. Despite mourning what you
Have lost. You find that your gain
Must come at a cost

Friends of Fur and Feather

WRITTEN BY ROMAN ZELENKA
ILLUSTRATED BY MADDIE WERNIG

In a land of giggles and sunshine so bright,
Lived a bunny named Sprite, fluffy and light.
In a meadow of flowers, colors so grand,
Sprite hopped and skipped across the soft sand.

Beyond the shore, lay an injured old owl,
At once, Sprite wrapped him with his nearby towel.
Taking him home, he tended to his new friend,
Cherishing every moment together they could spend.

Quickly healing, the old owl with feathers so wise,
Invited Sprite to learn 'neath the azure skies.
"Fly with me high," the owl sweetly cooed,
"Through clouds and rainbows, where dreams are pursued."

Sprite hopped onto his wise old friend's back,
Excited to experience what the owl had for a knack.
His owl friend soared with his wings open wide.
Sprite welcomed the wind and enjoyed the ride.

Together they soared, a duo so rare,
Through the sky, a pair beyond compare.
With laughter and joy, their friendship did grow,
In the skies above, a magical show.

The bunny and owl, in harmony's chime,
Dancing through clouds, creating stories in rhyme.
In this tale so sweet, where friendships take flight,
Children dream with delight, each and every night.

Seaside Wish

WRITTEN AND ILLUSTRATED BY SIENNA KUDERKA

Upon the coastal city of Carlsbad so fair,
Lived a girl named Maya, a delight so rare.
Dreams in her eyes and the ocean's roar,
Maya yearned to grow up and explore
Beyond the shore.

A mystical sprite with a bright glow,
Heard Maya's soft wish as soft winds blow.
On a moonlit beam, they soared high,
To a world of grown-ups beneath the sky.

Skyscraper tall, waves whispering near,
Maya saw, with a hint of a tear,
Grown life became her fear.
She missed the beach's embrace,
Wanting to disappear.

"I miss my giggles and friends so near,
Growing up brings a different cheer."
With a gentle shimmer, the fairy knew
To return to skies so true.

Back in time, by the moonlit bay,
Maya sighed, with dreams to stay.
In her heart, a childhood tide,
Maya stayed by her parent's side.

My Dream of Going to Japan

WRITTEN AND ILLUSTRATED BY
SUMMER NORRINGTON

Japan is like a different world. Sushi tastes like Something with a soft and salty flavor. Mochi tastes And almost feels like a soft marshmallow.

Onigiri tastes like sushi. Curry tastes like soup. Ramen tastes like pasta.

Dango tastes like mochi. Original Ramune drink tastes Like sparkling water and soda. Sando tastes like a Fruity cake or dessert. Gyoza looks and tastes like Fried dumplings on a stick. The Tokyo Tower almost Looks like the Eiffel Tower.

Tokyo looks like New York.

The cherry blossom trees look like pink Flower petals, falling from the tree.

Mount Fuji almost looks like a volcano. Japan looks like a safe country to visit.

The Little Stinker

WRITTEN AND ILLUSTRATED BY TANNER MOHR

In a cozy place, dreams
In my sight, I got a kitten,
All fluffy and light.

Midnight came, a surprise in
The air, little furball causing
A nighttime scare.

Litter box fights were a daily
Quest, tiny cat, making
Quite a mess.

Stinky poops, a room's
Delight, from Luna to Goose,
A name switch so right.

Endless nights with a
Lingering smell, winter
Allergies, I couldn't quite tell.

Three in the morning there
Was a sudden fright,
Diarrhea surprise,
Oh, what a night.

Cleanup rush, a bathroom
Race, poop everywhere,
What a disgrace.

Months later, the smell won't
Part. Even now, my love for
Goose won't depart.

WRITTEN BY VALY BEDOYA AND JULIYA TRICE
ILLUSTRATED BY FERNANDA BEDOYA

Under stormy skies, all dark and grey
Lightning struck where we usually play.

I looked outside, streets filled with rain,
Trees were swaying unstably; they looked in pain.

In my room, feeling quiet and bored,
Rainy weather made me snore.

Out the window, we took a glance,
Two wet bunnies we saw by chance.

Called our mom,
yet she was not near,
A mission for us,
with no fear.

We zipped our coats,
boots so snug,
Rainy weather
couldn't be a bug.

Grabbed umbrellas,
like Mary Poppins,
we flew,
To save the bunnies,
a task to pursue.

In the backyard,
the wind was so strong,
Umbrellas up,
we danced along.

In the rain, we go on a quest,
To help the bunnies and do our best.

Rock, paper, scissors, my sister won,
To pick up bunnies is scary but fun.

She reached towards them doubtfully,
And picked them up frightfully.

They came off the ground
but their heads didn't.
Quite a scary incident.

Headless bunny,
the closer we lean,
Not bunnies at all,
just rocks we've seen.

As we kicked them,
they made a clonking
sound, disappointed,
back to the house
we were bound.

Inside we went,
our quest was done,
Bunnies or rocks,
we had some fun.

Our hearts so light,
A rainy day turned
forever bright.

A Day On the Mountain

WRITTEN AND ILLUSTRATED BY FINN WILLIX

To the lift, I get to the first tracks,
Set my board down to get strapped.
As I tighten my bindings, they start to click.
Now, it is time to get on the lift.
The chair buzzes on the ride to the top.
The wind whips through me as I come to a stop.
Between the trees, the snow is deep.
I want to ride there, but it needs to be steep.
Or else I'll get stuck and have to unstrap,
In knee-deep snow, to make the trek back.

After walking a while, I finish the run.
And get on the lift. See, I'm not done.
This time, I won't ride through the trees.
In the park, I'll show off my steez.
Doing sick spins and sliding on rails,
Racing past all of these seeming like snails.
They watch in awe as I drop off a cliff,
Thinking and wishing that they
Could do all my tricks.
Launching jumps,
Drops, and spins,
My energy and
Strength start
To thin.

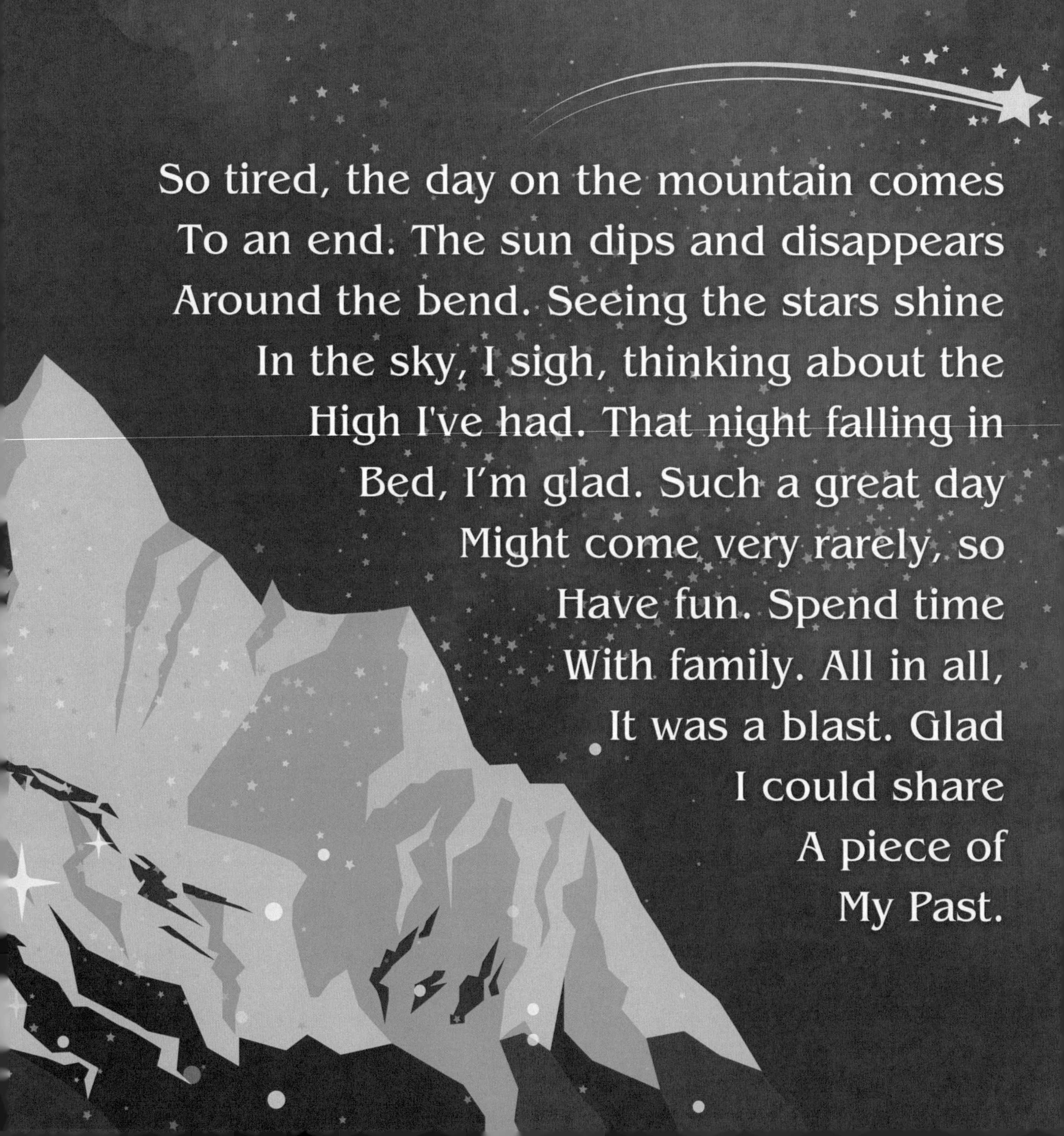

So tired, the day on the mountain comes
To an end. The sun dips and disappears
Around the bend. Seeing the stars shine
In the sky, I sigh, thinking about the
High I've had. That night falling in
Bed, I'm glad. Such a great day
Might come very rarely, so
Have fun. Spend time
With family. All in all,
It was a blast. Glad
I could share
A piece of
My Past.

My Baby, Mila

WRITTEN AND ILLUSTRATED BY
MAKAELA BARR

About the first time I set my eyes on Mila,
She was as beautiful and vibrant as a gardenia.

With so much energy and love to give,
She gave me the will to live.

In her eyes, the constant sparkle glows,
She even seems to sparkle on her nose.

When the two of us take a nap,
She turns me into a sap.

Of life, she seems to take every part of it in.
My baby, Mila, makes me feel like
I got the grand prize win.

Eleventh and Twelfth Grade

Adventures in a Magical Land

WRITTEN BY ALEXANDRA TEMME
ILLUSTRATED BY ALEXANDRA TEMME
AND MACKENZIE LUKIN

Once upon a time, in a land full of magic,
Where fairies danced, and wizards were tragic,
Lived a brave young girl named Lily
With her loyal friend, a talking daisy.

In this enchanted land, dreams came true,
And every day was a great adventure, too.
Lily and Daisy set off on a quest,
They headed down the flower-lined trail,
To find the golden key to unlock the treasure chest.

They journeyed through forests,
Tall trees and green,
Where the moonlight cast a blue
And purple, mystical sheen.

Lily and Daisy met a mischievous gnome,
Even with his red hat, he was oh so small,
Mr. Gnome decided to be nice, leading all alone,
The three of them to a hidden but tall waterfall.

With a leap of faith, over the crystal blue stream,
They entered a dark, dark cave as if in a dream,
There were no bats, monsters, or screams,
Only glittering crystals, lighting the way with beams.

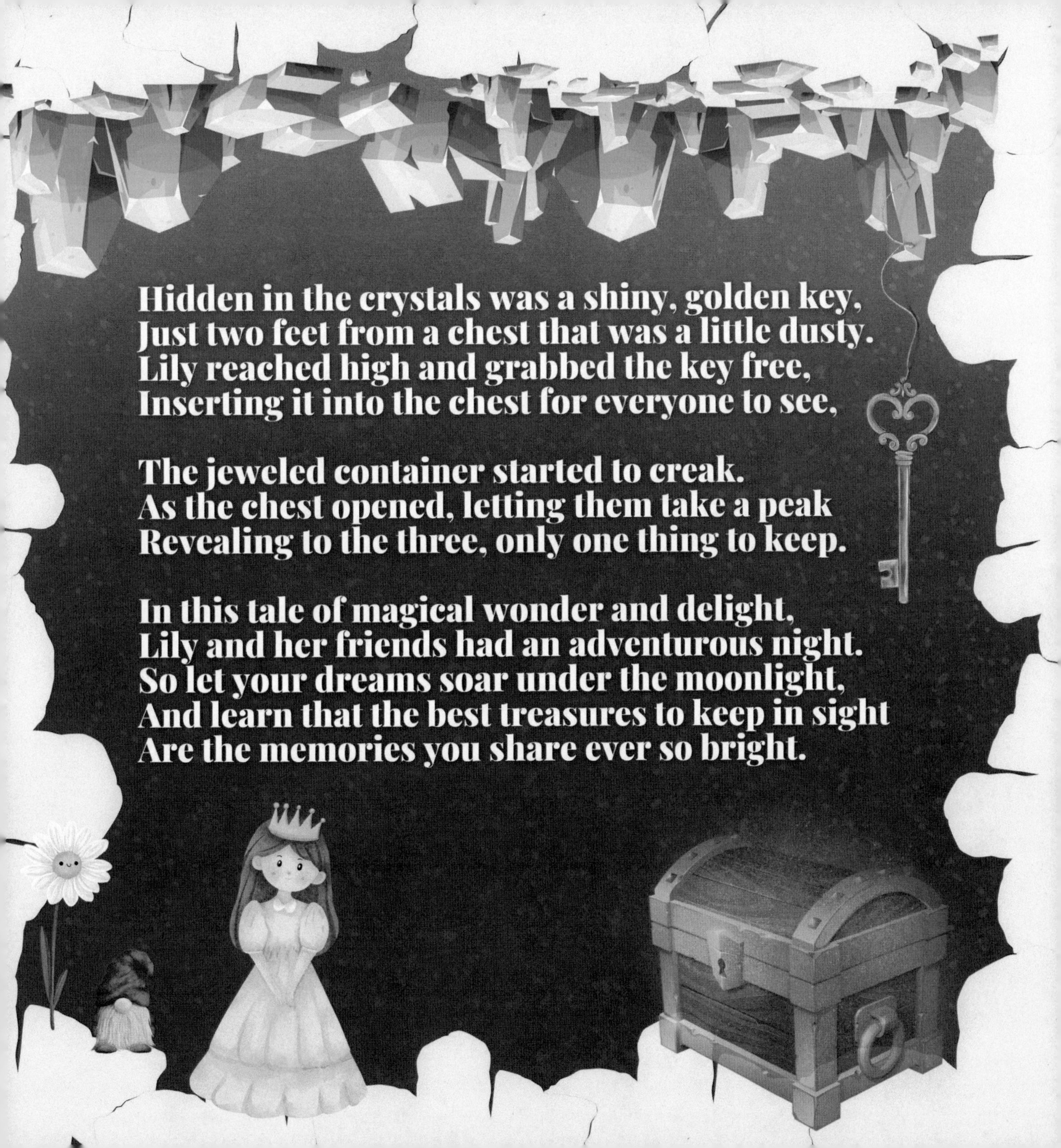

Hidden in the crystals was a shiny, golden key,
Just two feet from a chest that was a little dusty.
Lily reached high and grabbed the key free,
Inserting it into the chest for everyone to see,

The jeweled container started to creak.
As the chest opened, letting them take a peak
Revealing to the three, only one thing to keep.

In this tale of magical wonder and delight,
Lily and her friends had an adventurous night.
So let your dreams soar under the moonlight,
And learn that the best treasures to keep in sight
Are the memories you share ever so bright.

Fred the Friendly Furry Spider

WRITTEN BY BRADLEY BROWN
ILLUSTRATED BY EILISH FRIESTMAN

FRED IS A TINY, FURRY SPIDER.
FRED LIKES TO THREAD HIS WEB.
IT IS AS THIN AS A WIRE.
FRED ASPIRES TO HAVE MANY FRIENDS.
BUT NOBODY WANTS TO BE FRIENDS
WITH A SCARY SPIDER, SO FRED
FINALLY DECIDES TO DESCEND.

DETERMINED TO MAKE A FRIEND,
FRED GOES ON A JOURNEY.
WHILE DANGLING ON HIS THREAD, HE SAW
SOMETHING AHEAD.
ANOTHER SPIDER ON HIS THREAD!
OH BOY, I'VE FINALLY FOUND
A FRIEND! FRED SAID.

AS HE GOT CLOSER,
SO DID THE OTHER SPIDER,
BUT ONLY THEN, DID FRED REALIZE
IT WAS A MIRROR.
FRED WAS READY TO CALL IT QUITS, AND
JUST THREAD HIS WEB.

GOING BACK HOME, FRED HEARD A STRANGE BUZZ.
NOT WANTING TO GET ATTACKED, HE HURRIED IN A RUSH.
BUT AS HE GOT CLOSER, THE LOUD SOUND MADE HIM FLUSH.

WHEN FRED RETURNED HOME, HE WAS GREETED WITH A SURPRISE.
"A NEW FRIEND HAS FLOWN STRAIGHT INTO MY WEB!" FRED CRIED.
FRED PINCHED HIMSELF, THINKING IT MUST BE A DREAM.

HE UNSTICKS THE FLY FROM THE THREAD AND SAYS HIS NAME IS FRED.
THE FLY RESPONDS THAT HER NAME IS FIONA, AND ASKS FRED WHY HE HAS NO FRIENDS.

NOBODY WANTS TO BE FRIENDS WITH A SCARY SPIDER. EVERYONE RUNS AWAY, SAYING THEY HAVE NO DESIRE.

Pirate McKraken and Pirate McDavey were best friends!
They did everything together! Then, one day, their crew split up.
"You're your own captains now," their captain had told them.
So, the best friends had to say goodbye.
"Goodbye, Captain Davey!" said Captain McKraken
"Goodbye, Captain McKraken!" said Captain Davey.

Captain McKraken got to go on lots of
Adventures and find lots of treasures.
He missed his buddy a lot, though.
Then, one day, a bottle fell from the sky.
Bonk! It hit Captain McKraken
On the head. Inside the bottle
Was a scroll of paper.
"What message could be inside?"
Captain McKraken wondered.

It was a letter from Captain Davey!
He was sailing all around the globe!
And he had won a prize at a traveling circus.
It was a special crow that could find a best
Friend anywhere!

Captain McKraken was excited. Now he could
Write letters to his best friend!
"I'm searching for a magic red ruby. It's for
Lover Lou. She won't join me because
Being a pirate is dangerous," he wrote.
"If I have this magic gem, it will protect her
From the storms and sea monsters."

"I know where that gem is!" Captain
Davey exclaimed.
He drew a treasure map leading to where
The ruby was buried.
Captain McKraken couldn't believe his luck!
He followed the map and found the magic ruby!

"Thank you! Thank you!" he wrote to Captain Davey. "Now, Lou and I can be together!"
Captain McKraken waited for another letter, but the crow Never came back. "Where could Captain McDavey have Gone?" Lover Lou wondered.
Captain McKraken didn't know. He re-read the last letter. "I'm going to Pufferfish Coast to find treasure," Captain McDavey had told him.

Captain McKraken and Lover Lou sailed to Pufferfish Coast. They looked all over the beach for him, but he was nowhere to Be found. Finally, they stumbled upon a cave.
"Captain Davey might be inside!"
Captain McKraken shouted.

There was a HUGE pile of treasure inside!
Captain Davey was sitting on top of it.
"My hook is made out of shiny gold," he said.
"So the giant beast put me into the pile and
Kept me trapped here!

Just then, the beast stirred from its slumber.
"Grrr...that's my stuff," it growled.
"Uh oh! What are we going to do?"
Captain McKraken cried out!
"I'll take care of this gold boarder,"
Said Lover Lou. Then, kapow!
She karate kicked the beast and
Knocked it out.

Lover Lou ran up to Captain Davey and hugged him. "Thank you for making
It possible for Captain McKraken and me to be together," she whispered.
"Bah! Anything for my good ol' mate," Captain Davey said proudly.
The trio boarded their ship, off to have many more adventures together.

Friends To The Rescue

WRITTEN AND ILLUSTRATED BY
CHARLOTTE CLIFF AND
ERIN OSWALT

Juliet lived in a small red house on a large field. Her family raised chickens and sheep and housed many stray cats. One cold winter morning, the chicks ran out of food. They clucked and cried for something to eat. Juliet said, "I know what to do!" and gave the hungry chickens some of her own breakfast oats.

A few days later, she heard a lamb calling for help. He was lost in the tall grass and could not find his way back to his mother. She said, "I know what to do!" and led the lamb back to the other sheep on the other side of the farm. The next week, a stray cat, who was due to give birth any day, was looking for a place to have her kittens, but the ground was rough and freezing. When Juliet noticed, she said, "I know what to do!" and led the cat to her warm, sheltered barn. The cat found a pile of hay and made it into a bed for her kittens to sleep in.

Spring came around and Juliet was hopping from rock to rock at the edge of the large field when her foot slipped and she twisted her ankle. She cried for help, but no one heard her. She was hungry, cold, and all alone. "I don't know what to do!" she said.

Right when she was about to lose hope, a little chick brought her a sprig of berries to eat. Soon after, the little lamb came and laid beside her to keep her warm. After a few minutes, she finally saw her father walking toward her, following a cat and her five kittens. Since the animals remembered the good deeds Juliet had done for them, they helped her when she was in need.

Up and Over the Far View

WRITTEN AND ILLUSTRATED BY EILISH FRIESTMAN

Over the valley,
Through the breeze that blows on the grass.
Near the stream, inside the green,
Lies the home of Llidae.

Below the trees, there is she.
Upon the dirt where she sits,
Llidae is filled with unease.
For she dreams of seeing the sea.

Except Llidae is unprepared because she did not dare.
Beyond the stream, there might be all sorts of snares.
Out there may be frogs, wasps, spiders, or dragonflies.
Throughout her life, she had never seen but was nonetheless despaired.
After all, she doesn't know what's ahead, which fills her with dread.

Like moths to flame, the sea pulls her in, but Llidae is unlike moths.
Since she refuses to even contemplate a strike, simply is not the type.
Within its gripes, she has heard tales of the sea,
The salty air, and the push and pull of the tide.
Inside she cannot describe,
Her heart cried at being denied, such a divide, mind? heart?
Until she had finally arrived and decided to put her fear aside.

Past the valley, she doesn't know what's out there.
Yet she sits there, considering without tears,
Breathing for what feels like the first time.
Except doubt still lies, the wish clawed, but Llidae was scared.

Inside she was decided, already having been ignited,
Feelings cannot be uninvited.
Regarding what this applied here, Llidae concluded: she would go.
Fear collided but an answer was provided.
When she had finally subsided.
On she went, unguided but delighted;
She was finally going to gaze upon the sea.

Beyond uncharted terrain lies greatness.
Against the weight, Llidae chose not to be afraid.
Despite the way it invades,
Llidae is brave and attempts to be unphased.
Within her there are flames, but soon enough it will rain.
By leaving her home a trade is made,
And the blade is shaved.
Above, standing, remade.
Underneath, however, her fear remains.
After she ceased to entertain this fear,
Llidae attained much more than she aimed.
Above what she thought she could ever sustain.
Without the chain, she let the fire feign.
Past this, Llidae can obtain.
Absolutely anything in this plane.

BETWEEN THE PAGES

WRITTEN AND ILLUSTRATED BY JYNX PERKINS

Between the pages and between the lines.
Creating a path inside my mind.

Reaching out among the stars
I travel afar to space.

Beyond the vast expanse of empty space,
I search the skies in ceaseless chase.

From planet to planet.
To worlds one of a kind.
Traveling deep, below ocean currents,
To depths inside my mind.

Through the star systems, galaxies away,
The sea links in an intricate sort of way.

Memories recalled,
Something unable to grasp.
Something that I reach out,
And hope to clasp.

Within the constellations of thought,
I find I was lost inside my mind.
Instead of traveling out to space,
I was spacing out once again.

The Cat in the City

WRITTEN AND ILLUSTRATED BY LEILA MUELLER AND SAYLA STERN

Down the alleyway and
Through the bustling street,
Trots the brown tabby cat,
Along the concrete.

Cat does not fear anything at
All; not the roaring cars, nor
The buildings, standing tall.
Even the bravest of dogs are
Afraid of him, after all.
But come nightfall, when the
Hustling crowds begin to rest
There lies Cat, not feeling
Quite his best.

When all his friends travel
Home, Cat has just about
Nowhere to go.

Until this very evening,
When along comes little
Lacy, with a sudden
Greeting, that makes Cat
Think she's crazy.

Before he even has time
To blink, Cat has been
Transported to a big,
New, cozy room, unsure
What to think.

Soon enough, he is drinking
Fresh water from a bowl, and
Sleeping on a bed bigger than
An elephant whole!

While he stares out the
Window at the stars and city
Lights so happily, Cat thinks,
Yeah, I could get used to this
New life and loving family.

The Love Bug's Dance

WRITTEN AND ILLUSTRATED BY MALIAH KHAN

In a green garden, where sunbeams play,
A love bug danced through the light of day.

Spreading warmth,
Goodwill in its trace,
With radiant joy
And a caring grace.

As the love bug fluttered, a friend to all below,
Its wings painted in hues of passion, it treated
Every creature with gentle compassion.

One day it met a stink bug, unkind,
With sharp remarks and a bitter mind.
But the love bug,
Unfazed by the harsh sting,
Wrapped the stink bug
In friendship's wing.

Through patience and love,
The Love Bug's art
Softened the stink bug's
Once icy heart.
Now side by side, they danced anew,
A tale of transformation, love that grew.

THE GOLDEN HOUR

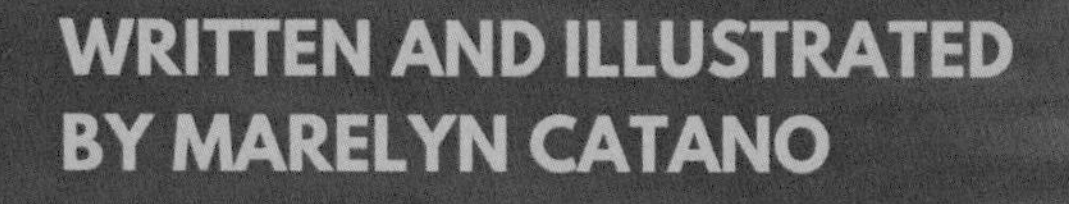

WELCOME

Through the gate, down the hall,
Inside the colorful classroom, I feel small.
Eyes wide, heart beating fast,
Hearing gibberish words leaves me downcast.

Among the snow-like skin and the hair strands of gold,
With milk chocolate skin and licorice-like hair, I grow cold.

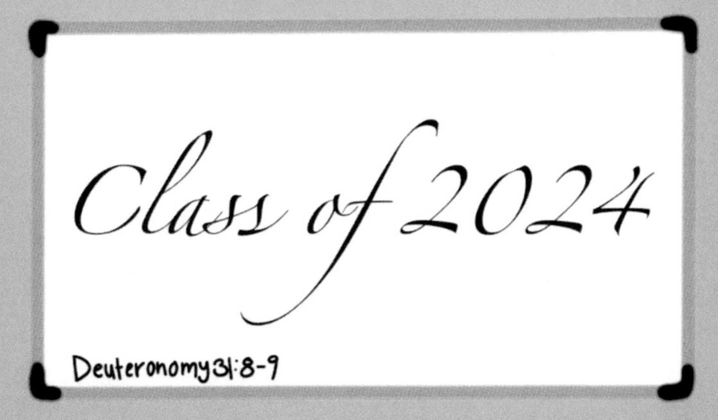

All eyes are on me, the girl twirling her hair,
Who knows nothing and is afraid no one will care.

Year after year, working harder than most,
Behind I started, but gave my utmost.

Determined to learn, I lost the fear of asking for assistance,
And found myself stronger with an abundance of persistence.

Now, my future looks brighter than the golden hour,
My sky has no limit, thanks to God, who is my power.

Dale the Whale

WRITTEN BY PRESTON DAU AND ILLUSTRATED BY TREVOR MARTINEZ, JACK SHAVER, AND JAYCE YOUNG

Beyond the surf, beneath the waves, a magical tale unfolds,
Of Dale the mighty grey whale so brave and bold.
Through whispering waves and oceans vast and deep,
Dale embarks on his migration,
Following currents that swirl and sweep.

From the chilliest waters to the warmest seas,
Dale travels far and wide, following his senses and the breeze.
Through ocean waters, alone on his voyage,
His story is of power, stamina, and most of all courage.

Continuing through moonlit nights and stormy strife,
Dale faces challenges of those who live the ocean life.
Beneath the surface where predators are unseen,
A journey long and lonely, many dangers convene.

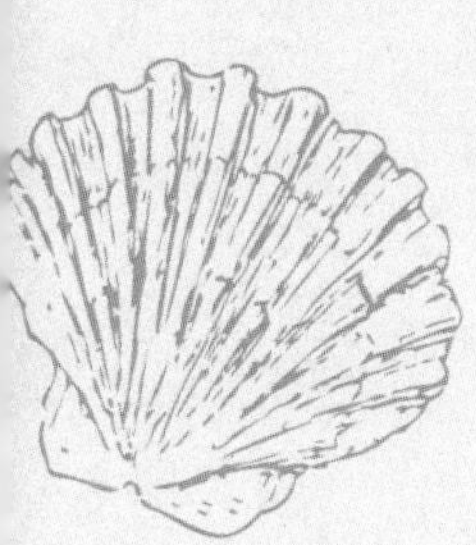

With his mighty tail's powerful whack,
Dale leaves a trail, knowing no way to turn back.
From icy chills of Arctic waters to bays of the Baja seas,
This annual crusade won't be completed with ease.

In the vastness of the ocean, feeling wild and free,
Dale encounters a pod of orcas further out to sea.
Their sleek black silhouettes make for a daunting sight.
A challenge arises for Dale in the stark of night.

Dale, unfazed, swims on to their coordinated attack.
With courage and strength, he's able to fight back.
The orcas, the most intelligent mammals on earth
Begin to converge, but Dale is ready to give them
What they deserve.

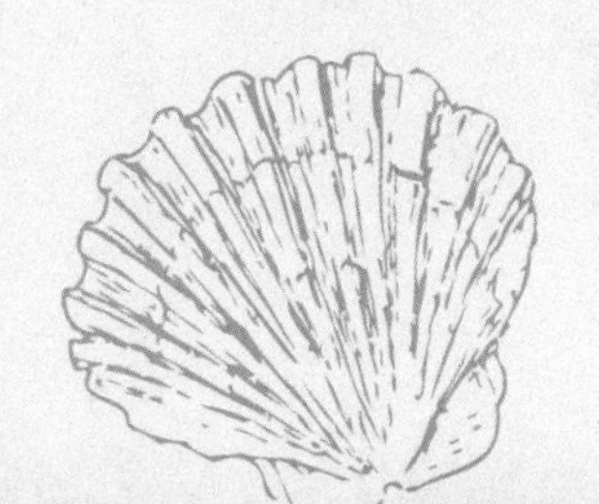

The orcas reluctantly give in and retreat,
This time defeated, still searching for something to eat.
Continuing through open waters on his journey to sunny bays,
He swims onward until he finds himself in the sun's warm rays.

At last in the distance, signs of beautiful Baja appear,
A destination cherished by many, drawing so near.
Now Dale, finally triumphant in his odyssey's quest,
Can finally rest in the warmth, his journey's best.

In the turquoise water of Baja so grand,
Dale finds peace in the ocean with the golden sand.
His tale is of triumph, such a legend to share,
In the heart of the magnificent ocean,
He continues without a care.

Sixth Grade Scaries

WRITTEN AND ILLUSTRATED BY ANTONIA LUISO

Up and about,
Before the sun was out,
From the window a ton of snow,
In the orange sky, started to glow.

Mom was awake and
Ready to bake.
The delicious smell was
One that only she could
Make.

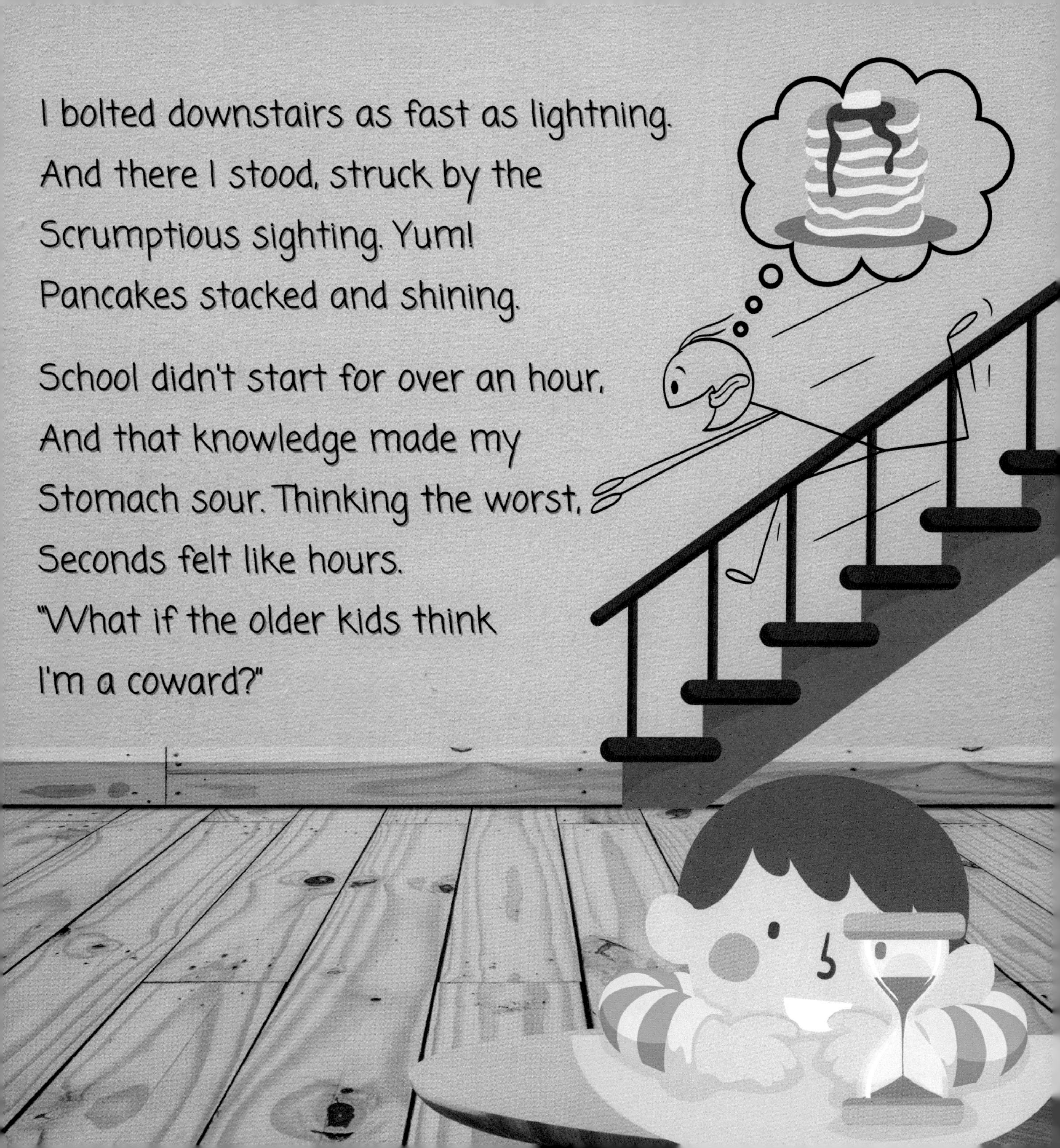

I bolted downstairs as fast as lightning.
And there I stood, struck by the
Scrumptious sighting. Yum!
Pancakes stacked and shining.

School didn't start for over an hour,
And that knowledge made my
Stomach sour. Thinking the worst,
Seconds felt like hours.
"What if the older kids think
I'm a coward?"

But my marvelous Mom
Shared stories about her first
Day of sixth grade.
And little by little, I began to
Feel cheerful, and less afraid.

My excitement grew as time flew.
Through Mom's teary eyes, I just
Knew. When she kissed me
Goodbye, I'd be blue.

But not for long because with
Each stride, I walked with
More and more pride.
And soon enough, all my
Troubles were set aside.
As it happened, middle school
Was not what I imagined.

No scary teachers, no
Dragons, no kids that
Were mean.
No, middle school
Turned out to be
Nothing but a dream as
I became part of the
Sixth grade team.

Colors of Love

WRITTEN AND ILLUSTRATED BY MAKAYLA SANTON

In a world of black and white
Lived two crayons, bold and bright.
Scarlet red and Violet hue
Colors vivid, pure, and true.

In a box, so plain and stark
They colored rainbows in the dark.
Their world was shades of grey and bland
But together, they made a vibrant land.

The black and white, in lines so straight
Couldn't see the love they'd create.
"Colors mustn't mix," they'd often say,
But Scarlet and Violet found their way.

Hand in hand, they'd dance and twirl
Creating swirls in a monochrome world.
Their love, a masterpiece, so bold and free,
A spectrum of what the world could be.

The others watched, at first unsure
But soon they saw something pure.
The beauty in the colors' blend
Made even the monochrome extend.

For love, they learned, is more than hue,
It's in the hearts of me and you.
Scarlet and Violet, in their dance,
Taught the world to take a chance.

To see beyond the black and white
To find the beauty in the light.
In a world that was once just night and day
The colors of love showed a new way.

So now, in the box where they reside
No color is ever pushed aside.
Together they color outside the lines
In a world where love beautifully entwines.

Seventh Grade Contributors

"Each student's story represents them in one way."

Gwen Daynes

- Aaron Love believes reading unlocks the door to your imagination that could never have been explored otherwise.
- Gwen Daynes likes to go to the beach and surf with family and friends.
- Keira Segal is a dancer who has been dancing since eighteen-months-old and loves to perform.
- Thomas Sullivan enjoys hanging out with friends.
- Willow Anderson loves snowboarding with her sister, but she also enjoys going to the beach.

Eighth Grade Contributors

"With many funny, thrilling, and amazing short stories, this book is just for you!"

Jack Houlihan

- Benjamin Hansink and Paige McConnell love all animals.
- Brooklyn Payne's favorite park is over the hill.
- Carter Dau thinks if you change the way you look at things, the things you look at will change.
- Emma Boll loves playing lacrosse.
- Jack Houlihan loves spending his day at the beach surfing.
- Jordy Novell likes to spend time at the beach with friends.
- Max Olschewski loves to play football and fish.
- Rebekah Sarris thinks life is a roller coaster, but with support, we can find the ups.
- Sammy Yosufi enjoys sketching, baking, watching classic movies, playing video games, collecting stamps, and solving puzzles.

Freshman Contributors

"Enjoy this collection of lighthearted, funny, and memorable stories written by Carlsbad Seaside Academy students."

Channah Burgoyne

- Autumn Norrington likes drawing and the arts.
- Channah Burgoyne believes that nothing is impossible.
- Everett Castaneda enjoys playing soccer.
- Felix Bueno enjoys surfing and playing *Battlefield* with his friends.
- Finn Willis enjoys snowboarding, surfing, and biking.
- Holland Fuller is a surfer and water polo player.
- Julieta Pareja loves to read books and play tennis.
- Kaleb Miller enjoys hanging with friends and going to the desert.
- Katy Medway enjoys reading stories and listening to music.
- Keira Sweeney enjoys baking and watching sunsets.
- Makaela Barr enjoys the snow and listening to music.
- Nate Weitz likes skating with friends and surfing.
- Roman Zelenka wrestles for Carlsbad High School.
- Sienna Kuderka believes chasing dreams is as important as the final destination.
- Summer Norrington dreams of going to Japan.
- Ty Shaver likes the ocean and is fascinated with nature.

Sophomore Contributors

“The Seaside Storybook is an enchanting collection of children's tales filled with whimsy, friendship, and adventure.”

Valy Bedoya

- Cash Watson likes surfing and having fun with friends.
- Cruz Douglass enjoys fostering cats.
- Hannah Carroll believes time spent with family and friends creates the most valuable memories you will ever have.
- Jacob Kahane encourages that waves empower your inner brave.
- Joshua Sherman enjoys listening to music and hanging out with friends.
- Lily Irvine enjoys hanging out at the beach and listening to music.
- Luke Macbeth enjoys surfing and going to Mexico with his cousins.
- Maizie Zarling enjoys art, writing, and dance.
- Tanner Mohr enjoys listening to music and going to the beach.
- Valy Bedoya and Juliya Trice believe in expressing creativity and sharing imagination.

Junior/Senior Contributors

**“In the Seaside town of Carlsbad,
an imaginative group of adventure-seeking
kids departed on a magical journey.”**

Mackenzie Lukin

- Alexandra Temme and Mackenzie Lukin believe making memories is the most important part of life.
- Bradley Brown likes writing stories for everyone to enjoy.
- Cassie Noble is a sucker for stories about the power of friendship.
- Charlotte Cliff and Erin Oswalt encourage others to treat others the way they want to be treated.
- Eilish Friestman believes people develop resilience and experience personal growth by challenging fear head-on.
- Jynx Perkins enjoys reading stories and can often be found lost in them.
- Leila Mueller hopes to inspire others that life will continue to get better.
- Makayla Santon enjoys advocating for others.
- Maliah Kahn encourages others to do everything in love.
- Marelyn Catano likes helping other people.
- Preston Dau, Jack Shaver, Trevor Martinez, and Jayce Young’s motto is to enjoy life to the fullest.
- Sayla Stern encourages others to find passion and peace in life.
- Toni Luiso's lifelong goal is to ignite joy in others!

Mrs. Ryan/Former Student Contributors

Whether you're fighting a fear, pursuing a passion, dreaming of adventure, or just love reading, you can find something for yourself within these colorful pages! The Seaside Storybook is a great reminder for kids and parents of just how strong they truly are."

Emma Stokes

- Brooklyn Dillion acknowledges that change is a difficult concept.
- Emma Stokes takes time to help others see their worth, so send that note, give a high-five, and compliment others.
- Maddie Wernig loves writing as a creative outlet and believes a single person can make a difference!
- Noah Mendles Elliott likes playing basketball and writing stories.
- Mrs. Ryan believes every student has unlimited potential.

THANK YOU FOR READING
THE SEASIDE STORYBOOK

Made in the USA
Las Vegas, NV
05 April 2024